Sports Illustrated KIDS

GRAPHIC NOVELS

STONE ARCH BOOKS
a capstone imprint

STRIKERS' SUPERSTAR HIDES FROM SPOTLIGHT

CARLOS RAMIREZ

STATS:
AGE: 14
TEAM: STRIKERS
POSITION: STRIKER

BIO: Carlos Ramirez impresses everyone with his lightning-fast reflexes, flashy kicks, and sneaky passes. He's a shoo-in for starting forward on varsity next year, and his grades are picture perfect. There's just one thing holding him back: when the pressure's on, Carlos prefers to be off the field. If this young star hopes to shine, he'll have to learn how to thrive in the spotlight.

UP NEXT: SPOTLIGHT STRIKER

TOU YANG

AGE: 14 TEAM: STRIKERS
POSITION: MIDFIELD

BIO: Tou is a small midfielder, but he has the confidence of a giant. When everyone else is ready to give up, Tou keeps their chins up, and their eyes on the ball. He is Carlos's best bud on and off the field.

BLZ vs BKS
3-1
TGR vs ROR
33-32
EAG vs BAN
14-7
SPA vs WLD
4-3
BAN vs ROR
21-15
ROR vs LIG
4-3
BLZ vs BKS
3-1

RAMÓN RAMIREZ

AGE: 34
BIO: Ramón is a professional soccer player from Mexico. He hopes that his nephew, Carlos, will one day follow in his footsteps.

RAMIREZ

COACH DANIELS

AGE: 38   **TEAM: STRIKERS**
BIO: Coach Daniels expects team unity and hard work from all his Strikers. To him, giving it everything you've got is all that matters.

COACH

MARTA RAMIREZ

AGE: 44
BIO: Mrs. Ramirez is Carlos's mother. Her younger brother, Ramón, is a big part of their lives.

MRS. RAMIREZ

PRESENTS

SPOTLIGHT STRIKER

A PRODUCTION OF

STONE ARCH BOOKS
a capstone imprint

written by Blake A. Hoena
illustrated by Gerardo Sandoval
colored by Benny Fuentes

designed and directed by Bob Lentz
edited by Sean Tulien
creative direction by Heather Kindseth
editorial direction by Michael Dahl

Sports Illustrated KIDS *Spotlight Striker* is published by Stone Arch Books,
151 Good Counsel Drive, P.O. Box 669, Mankato, Minnesota 56002.
www.capstonepub.com

Summary: Carlos Ramirez has always been the Strikers' best scorer. But
the state's best team is coming to town, and Carlos hears that he'll have
a very special fan in the stands. His uncle, a professional soccer player,
will be watching his nephew's every move during the Strikers' biggest
game of the year. As the pressure begins to set in, Carlos struggles to
even hit the ball. Everyone has seen that Carlos is a gifted athlete, but no
one knows whether he'll shine as the center of attention, or be blinded
by the spotlight.

Cataloging-in-Publication Data is available at the Library of Congress
website.

ISBN: 978-1-4342-2128-5 (library binding)
ISBN: 978-1-4342-2787-4 (paperback)

Printed in the United States of America in Stevens Point, Wisconsin.
102010   005977R

I could never do a bicycle kick during a game.

What? Why not?

It's easy when we're just messing around during practice.

But during a game, with everyone

You worry too much, Carlos.

Easy for you to say.

You don't have an uncle who plays professional soccer in Mexico.

Not *this* weekend. He's *here!* Uncle Ramón is coming to watch me play.

That's awesome!

No, Tou, you don't get it.

He's amazingly talented. A professional.

If I make even one mistake out there with him watching . . .

TWEEEEET!

SWWISHH!

GOAL, STRIKERS!!!

...but you should be proud of how you played tonight.

After the game...

Great game, you two!

I know it's not very rewarding when a game ends in a tie...

Thanks, Coach.

RAMIREZ

STRIKERS

SOCCER STAR STEPS UP AND SHINES IN THE SPOTLIGHT

BY THE NUMBERS

FINAL SCORE:
STRIKERS: 1
BANDITS: 1

GOALS:
RAMIREZ: 1
ROGERS: 1

STORY: Carlos Ramirez overcame his fears to lead the Strikers to a tie against the ultra-talented Bandits. Any doubts about Carlos's ability to perform under pressure were silenced with the resounding thud of his game-tying goal — and he even did it by way of an incredible bicycle kick! If today's game is any indication, the Strikers have a big season ahead of them.

POWERED BY **STONE ARCH**

BLZ vs BKS
3-1
TGR vs RDR
33-32
EAG vs BA
14-7
SPA vs WLI
4-3
BAN vs RDI
21-15
RDR vs LIG
4-3

SZ *POSTGAME EXTRA*

WHERE *YOU* ANALYZE THE GAME!

Soccer fans were served up a real surprise when the Strikers tied the Bandits in a heated matchup. Let's go into the stands and ask some fans about the day's events...

DISCUSSION QUESTION 1

What do you think about games that end in a tie? Does there always have to be a winner? Why or why not?

DISCUSSION QUESTION 2

Which character in this book is your favorite — Tou, Carlos, Uncle Ramón, or Coach Daniels? Why?

WRITING PROMPT 1

Carlos is nervous about playing in front of his uncle. When was the last time that you were nervous? What happened? Write about a nervous experience.

WRITING PROMPT 2

Carlos has a talented uncle. Do you have any skilled relatives? What have they done that is impressive? Write about your special family members and friends.

GLOSSARY

ASSIST (uh-SIST)—one or two passes that directly lead to a goal

BICYCLE KICK (BYE-si-kuhl KIK)—when a player kicks the ball over his head in mid-air with his back facing the ground

DEFENSEMEN (di-FENS-muhn)—players whose main task is to stop the opposing team from scoring

DRAW (DRAW)—a game that ends with a tied score

FORWARDS (FOR-wurdz)—players who are tasked with scoring most of their team's goals. They play in front of the rest of the team.

HEADER (HED-ur)—a kick or pass done with a player's head

MIDFIELDERS (MID-feel-durz)—players who link together the offense and defense of a team. They play behind forwards.

PENALTY KICK (PEN-uhl-tee KIK)—a kick taken from the penalty spot against the opposing goalie

STRIKER (STRYK-er)—a team's most talented forward who plays near the center of the field

CREATORS

BLAKE A. HOENA › *Author*

Blake A. Hoena grew up in central Wisconsin, where he wrote stories about trolls lumbering around in the woods behind his parent's house. Later, he moved to Minnesota to pursue a Masters in Creative Writing from Minnesota State University, Mankato. Since graduating, Blake has written more than thirty books for children, including graphic novel retellings of *The Legend of Sleepy Hollow* and the Perseus and Medusa myth, as well as *Kickoff Blitz*.

GERARDO SANDOVAL › *Illustrator*

Gerardo Sandoval is a professional comic book illustrator from Mexico. He has worked on many well-known comics including the Tomb Raider books from Top Cow Productions. He has also worked on designs for posters and card sets.

BENNY FUENTES › *Colorist*

Benny Fuentes lives in Villahermosa, Tabasco in Mexico, where it's just as hot as the sauce is. He studied graphic design in college, but now he works as a full-time colorist in the comic book industry for companies like Marvel, DC Comics, and Top Cow Productions. He shares his home with two crazy cats, Chelo and Kitty, who act like they own the place.

CHESTER COYOTE and CORA RAMIREZ IN:
PAINTBALL PUNK

Chester and Cora weren't seeing eye-to-eye...

Is everything a joke to you, Chester?

Oh, Chester — when will you grow up?! Why, when I was your age, I —

That's it! You're off the team!

Urk!

》》 LOVE THIS QUICK COMIC? READ THE WHOLE STORY IN PAINTBALL PUNK — ONLY FROM STONE ARCH BOOKS!

HOT SPORTS,

HOT

FORMAT

PAINTBALL PUNK

TULIEN / ABURTOV

Sports Illustrated KIDS
GRAPHIC NOVELS

SPORTS FICTION

AVALANCHE FREESTYLE

CIENCIN / ABURTOV

Sports Illustrated KIDS
GRAPHIC NOVELS

SPORTS FICTION

END ZONE THUNDER

CIENCIN / SANDOVAL

Sports Illustrated KIDS
GRAPHIC NOVELS

SPORTS FICTION

SHOT CLOCK SLAM

KREIE / ABURTOV

Sports Illustrated KIDS
GRAPHIC NOVELS

SPORTS FICTION

SKATEBOARD BREAKDOWN

FEIN / SANDOVAL

Sports Illustrated KIDS
GRAPHIC NOVELS

SPORTS FICTION

GREAT CHARACTERS BATTLE FOR SPORTS GLORY IN TODAY'S HOTTEST FORMAT—GRAPHIC NOVELS!

ONLY FROM STONE ARCH BOOKS

Sports Illustrated KIDS
GRAPHIC NOVELS